GIVE A DOG A BONE

Stories, Poems, Jokes, and Riddles About Dogs

Compiled by JOANNA COLE
and STEPHANIE CALMENSON

with original illustrations by
JOHN SPEIRS

SCHOLASTIC INC.
New York Toronto London Auckland Sydney

ISBN 0-590-46373-X

12 11 10 9 8 7 6 5 4 3 2 1   7 8 9/9 0 1 2/0

Printed in the U.S.A.   23

Designed by Claire Bowser Counihan

ACKNOWLEDGMENTS

"It Does Not Say Meow!" from IT DOES *NOT* SAY MEOW! AND OTHER ANIMAL RIDDLE RHYMES by Beatrice Schenk de Regniers. Copyright © 1972 by Beatrice Schenk de Regniers. Reprinted by permission of Clarion Books/Houghton Mifflin Co. All rights reserved.

"Who Is She?" by Stephanie Calmenson. Copyright © 1994 by Stephanie Calmenson. Reprinted by permission of the author.

"Puppies" by Jack Kent. Copyright © 1967 by the Estate of Jack Kent. Reprinted by permission.

"Home Sweet Home" by John Ciardi. Copyright The Ciardi Family Trust. Reprinted by permission.

"My Dog" by Max Fatchen from SONGS FOR MY DOG AND OTHER PEOPLE. Copyright © 1980 by Max Fatchen. Published by Kestrel Books and in Puffin Books.

"Shaggy Dog" by Stephanie Calmenson. Copyright © 1994 by Stephanie Calmenson. Reprinted by permission of the author.

"Retriever" by Joanna Cole. Copyright © 1994 by Joanna Cole. Reprinted by permission of the author.

"Sunning" by James S. Tippett from CRICKETY CRICKET! THE BEST LOVED POEMS OF JAMES S. TIPPETT. Copyright © 1933 and renewed 1973 by Martha K. Tippett. Reprinted by permission of HarperCollins Publishers.

"Dog Dreams" by Stephanie Calmenson. Copyright © 1994 by Stephanie Calmenson. Reprinted by permission of the author.

"Making a Friend" by Myra Cohn Livingston from O SLIVER OF LIVER AND OTHER POEMS by Myra Cohn Livingston. Copyright © 1979 by Myra Cohn Livingston. Reprinted by permission of Marian Reiner for the author.

"Fido" by Stephanie Calmenson, illustrated by Maxie Chambliss. Text copyright © 1987 by Stephanie Calmenson. Illustrations copyright © 1987 by Maxie Chambliss. Reprinted by permission of Scholastic Inc.

"The Kittens" from HENRY AND MUDGE IN PUDDLE TROUBLE by Cynthia Rylant. Illustrated by Suçie Stevenson. Copyright © 1987 by Cynthia Rylant. Illustrations copyright © 1987 by Suçie Stevenson. Reprinted with permission of Simon & Schuster Children's Publishing Division.

"The Last Puppy" by Frank Asch. Copyright © 1989 by Frank Asch. Reprinted by permission of Simon & Schuster Children's Publishing Division.

"My Dog and the Knock Knock Mystery" by David A. Adler. Copyright © 1985 by David A. Adler. Reprinted by permission of David A. Adler.

"Barry: The Dog Who Saved People" from FIVE TRUE DOG STORIES by Margaret Davidson. Copyright © 1977 by Margaret Davidson. Reprinted by permission of Scholastic Inc.

"Give a Dog a Bone: Tail Ends" selected by Joanna Cole and Stephanie Calmenson. Copyright © 1996 by Joanna Cole and Stephanie Calmenson. Used by permission of the authors.

CONTENTS

IT DOES *NOT* SAY MEOW!

Poems

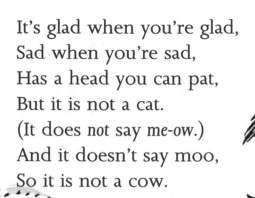

from IT DOES *NOT* SAY MEOW!
and Other Animal Riddle Rhymes

It's glad when you're glad,
Sad when you're sad,
Has a head you can pat,
But it is not a cat.
(It does *not* say me-ow.)
And it doesn't say moo,
So it is not a cow.

It says *woof* or *bow-wow*.
Does that sound like a frog?
No! It's a . . .

ȸop

Beatrice Schenk de Regniers

WHO IS SHE?

She's silly, snoopy,
Sometimes droopy,
Itchy, waggy,
Getting shaggy,
Licky, puddly,
Very cuddly,
Not much bigger
Than a cup.
Who is she?
She's my pup!

Stephanie Calmenson

PUPPIES

There were puppies on the sofa
    And puppies on the chairs
And puppies in the dining room
    And on the cellar stairs
There were cold ones on the icebox
    And hot ones near the stove
There were puppies by the pack and herd
    And puppies by the drove
There were puppies in the parlor
    And puppies in the hall

And puppies on the porch and roof
    And on the garden wall
There were puppies in the attic
    In the bedroom
In the den
    And even in the closets
There were puppies (nine or ten)
    "Look at all those puppies, Henry.
Aren't they just dear?"
    "Enjoy them while they're puppies, Jane.
They'll be full-grown dogs next year."

Jack Kent

HOME SWEET HOME

A flea on a pooch doesn't care
Which part it is crossing to where.
  Like mud to a frog,
  Any part of a dog
Suits a flea and it's glad to be there.

John Ciardi

MY DOG

My dog is such a gentle soul,
Although he's big it's true.
He brings the paper in his mouth.
He brings the postman too.

Max Fatchen

SHAGGY DOG

I have a shaggy dog named Rose.
She has hair that grows and grows
And grows and grows.
Past her eyes, past her nose,
It goes way down to her toes.
Can she see? I don't suppose—
Unless, of course, a big wind blows!

Stephanie Calmenson

RETRIEVER

One morning,
my pet mouse was gone.
I looked at the cage door,
the latch wasn't on.
I heard a rustle
and turned around to see
the papers in the corner—
that's where he must be.
I stepped across the room
to capture the mouse,
but I'd forgotten the dog—
the dog was in the house!
She'll eat it, I thought
and said, "Girl, get away!"
But she was already there,
I saw with dismay.

Her nose was her guide
to the hiding place.
In a second she rose
with a grin on her face,
the prey in her mouth,
the pink tail hanging out.
"Bad dog!" and "Drop it!"
I heard myself shout.
The dog looked at me,
her eyes soft and calm,
then peacefully, carefully
laid in my palm
the perfect, undamaged,
runaway mouse.
"Now there, aren't you glad
there's a dog in the house?"

Joanna Cole

9

SUNNING

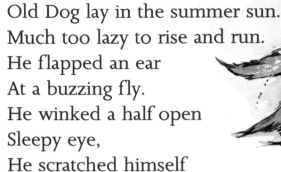

Old Dog lay in the summer sun.
Much too lazy to rise and run.
He flapped an ear
At a buzzing fly.
He winked a half open
Sleepy eye,
He scratched himself
On an itching spot,
As he dozed on the porch
Where the sun was hot.
He whimpered a bit
From force of habit
While he lazily dreamed
Of chasing a rabbit.
But Old Dog happily lay in the sun
Much too lazy to rise and run.

James S. Tippett

10

DOG DREAMS

Your eyes are closed
Your body still,
Except your paws
That race at will.

Where do you go, dog,
In your sleep?
Have you important
Appointments to keep?

Stephanie Calmenson

MAKING A FRIEND

He wouldn't come at first.
But when
I stood quite still a long time,
Then

His tail began to move.
His eyes
Looked into mine, and in
Surprise

He sort of sniffed and showed
His tongue.
Then, suddenly, he moved and
Sprung

To where I stood. He smelled
My feet
And came up close so we could
Meet.

So then, I gently stroked
His head.
"Good boy—I'll be your friend,"
I said.

He licked me then, and that
Was good,
Because it meant
He understood.

Myra Cohn Livingston

13

THE FIRST FRIEND

When the Man waked up he said,
"What is Wild Dog doing here?"
And the Woman said,
"His name is not Wild Dog anymore,
but the First Friend,
because he will be our friend
for always and always and always."

Rudyard Kipling

DOG TALES

Stories

Fido

by Stephanie Calmenson
pictures by Maxie Chambliss

Mr. Tinker and Fido look just alike.
When Mr. Tinker gets sick, he sends
Fido to work in his place.
Will anyone notice?

Mr. Tinker was the head of a large company that
made and sold things. He worked hard and sometimes
stayed at the office until late at night.

The workers liked Mr. Tinker. They thought he could
do no wrong.

When Mr. Tinker went home he was greeted by his loyal dog, Fido. Mr. Tinker and Fido did everything together.

When they went out, people stared at them. "That dog looks just like his master," they would say.

That made Fido very happy. He walked home with his head held high.

One day when Mr. Tinker's alarm clock went off, Mr.
Tinker did not jump up as usual. He did not feel well.

"Fido, I cannot go to work today," said Mr. Tinker.
"And there is an important meeting this morning. If
only you could go in my place."

Fido stood up and wagged his tail.

"Well, why not?" said Mr. Tinker. "You're a smart dog."

Mr. Tinker dressed
Fido in his best suit . . .

and fed him a hearty
breakfast.

Then he gave Fido a box
of dog biscuits for lunch
and told him how to get to
the office.

Take the bus at the corner.

As soon as Fido left,
Mr. Tinker went back to bed.

Fido had no trouble
getting to work.
He found his way to
Mr. Tinker's office
and sat down in
Mr. Tinker's chair.

"Good morning, sir,"
said Norman,
Mr. Tinker's assistant.
    "Woof!" said Fido.
    "Bad cold you have there,
Mr. Tinker. I'll get you
some tea," said Norman.

Fido liked the tea.
The phone rang.
Fido didn't like
the noise.

"Grr!" he said.
"I'll get that,"
said Norman.
"You should save
your voice today."

Norman listened, then said, "Ms. Potter wants to know where the meeting will be, sir."

"Woof! Woof!" said Fido.

"Room two," said Norman into the phone.

At half past nine, Fido had to go out for his morning walk. Norman went with him.

They went across the street. Fido ducked behind a bush.

"Nice day for picking flowers," said Norman.

Fido saw a cat and went after it.

"It's kind of you to try to help that cat, sir, but shouldn't we call the Animal Rescue Squad?" asked Norman.

Fido saw a poodle pass by. He started to chase her.

"It's almost time for the meeting, Mr. Tinker!"
Norman called.

Fido ran back to the office.

The workers were ready for the meeting.

"Woof!" said Fido, bringing the meeting to order.

Everyone got to work. They were trying to think of something new to make and sell. What Fido needed was flea powder.

"Itchy suit, sir?" whispered Norman.

"What about spinach lollipops?" asked a worker.

"Grrr," said Fido. He was hungry.

"You're right, sir," said the worker. "That wasn't a very good idea."

Fido took out his box of dog biscuits.

"Dog biscuits?" someone asked. "You think we should make dog biscuits?"

"That's a fine idea," said Norman.

Everyone agreed. After all, it was Mr. Tinker's idea, and Mr. Tinker could do no wrong.

Everyone was getting a pat on the back. Fido waited for his pat, too.

When he didn't get one, he tried all his best tricks.

You look tired sir, you should go home and rest.

That night, Mr. Tinker greeted Fido at the door and gave him an extra-good dinner.

"Thank you, Fido," he said. "I feel much better."

The next day, Norman was glad to see Mr. Tinker looking like his old self.

"We've started work on the dog biscuits. That was one of your best ideas!" Norman said.

"Why, yes, I guess it was," said Mr. Tinker.

"We'll need a picture of a dog for the box. Don't you have a dog, sir?" asked Norman.

Soon Fido's Tasty Treats were in all the stores. They were the best-selling dog biscuits on the market. Mr. Tinker was very proud of Fido.

People still stared at Mr. Tinker and Fido. But instead of saying, "That dog looks just like his master," now they said, "That man looks just like his dog!"

That made Mr. Tinker very happy. He walked home
with his head held high.

The Kittens

by Cynthia Rylant
pictures by Suçie Stevenson

Henry's big dog, Mudge, makes friends
with some new kittens. Then a mean dog
comes along and the kittens are in danger!

In May the cat who lived

next door to Henry and Mudge

had a litter of kittens.

There were five kittens.

One was orange.

One was gray.

One was black and white.

And two were all black.

The kittens sometimes stayed
in a box in their front yard
to get some sun
while the mother cat rested.
One day Henry and Mudge
peeked in the box.
They saw tiny little
kitten faces
and tiny little
kitten paws
and heard tiny little
kitten meows.

Mudge sniffed
and sniffed and sniffed.
He wagged his tail
and sneezed
and sniffed some more.
Then he put his
big head into the box
and with his big tongue
he licked
all five kittens.

Henry laughed.
"Do you want
some kittens of your own?"
he asked Mudge.
Mudge grunted
and wagged his tail again.
Whenever the kittens
were in their front yard,
Henry and Mudge
visited the box.
Henry loved their
little noses.
And he had even
given them names.

He called them
Venus,
Earth,
Mars,
Jupiter,
and Saturn.
Henry loved planets, too.

While Henry was at school one day,
a new dog came up Henry's street.
The five kittens
were sleeping
in the box in their yard.
Mudge was sleeping in Henry's house.

When the new dog
got closer to Henry's house,
Mudge's ears went up.

When the new dog
got even closer
to Henry's house,
Mudge's nose went in the air.
And just when the new dog
was in front of
Henry's house,
Mudge barked.

He barked and barked
and barked
until Henry's mother
opened the door.

And just as
Mudge ran out the door,
the new dog
was in the neighbor's yard,
looking in the kittens' box.
And just as the new dog
was putting his big teeth into the box,
Mudge ran up behind him.

SNAP! went Mudge's teeth
when the new dog saw him.
SNAP! went Mudge's teeth again
when the new dog looked back
at the box of kittens.

Mudge growled.

He looked into the eyes of the new dog.

He stood ready to jump.

And the new dog backed away
from the box.

He didn't want the kittens anymore.

He just wanted to leave.

And he did.

Mudge looked in the kitten box.
He saw five tiny faces
and five skinny tails
and twenty little paws.
He reached in and licked
all five kittens.

Then he lay down
beside the box
and waited for Henry.
Venus,
Earth,
Mars,
Jupiter,
and Saturn
went back to sleep.

The Last Puppy

story and pictures by Frank Asch

There is one puppy who is always last.
Will anyone want him?

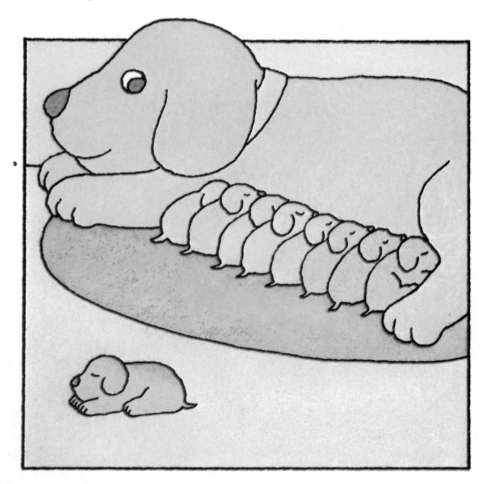

I was the last of Momma's nine puppies.

The last to eat from Momma,

the last to open my eyes,

the last to learn to drink milk

from a saucer,

and the last one into
the doghouse at night.
I was the last puppy.

One day Momma's owner put up a sign:
PUPPIES FOR SALE.

The next day, a little girl came
and took one of us away.
That night I couldn't sleep very well.
I kept wondering:
When will my turn come?
Will I be the last puppy again?

In the morning, a little boy
came to choose a puppy.
"Take me, take me!" I barked.
"That puppy's too noisy," he said,
and picked another puppy instead.

woof!

Later that day, a nice lady from
the city almost picked me.
But when I tried to jump into
her lap, she fell backwards
right into our bowl of milk.

When a farmer and his family
came to choose a puppy,
I got so excited when
the farmer picked me up,
I bit him on the nose.
They picked two puppies,
leaving four of us behind.

Soon there were just three of us left.
Then two,

then just me, the last puppy.

But one day, my turn came, too.
Big hands picked me up
and gave me to a little boy.
We got into a car
and drove away.

The little boy held me on his lap.
He put his face down close to mine
and I licked him on the nose.

He laughed and said,
"You know what?
You're my first puppy."

My Dog and the Knock Knock Mystery

by David A. Adler
pictures by John Speirs

Jennie's dog solves mysteries! What's that strange knocking
on Billy's door? Jennie and My Dog take the case.

My name is Jennie. This is my dog. My dog has white curly hair,
lots of spots, a long tail and is really smart. She solves mysteries.

I couldn't think of a good name for my dog, so I just call her
My Dog.

One morning, I was sitting on the porch reading a book about cats.
My Dog wasn't reading with me. She doesn't like cats. My Dog was
playing with a toy bone.

Then My Dog poked me with her nose. I looked up and saw Billy Jones. He was standing on the porch steps.

"I need you to help me solve a mystery," Billy said, yawning.

Billy sat next to me. He sat on My Dog's toy bone. As soon as Billy sat down, My Dog poked him.

I said to Billy, "My Dog wants you to tell us about the mystery."

Billy laughed. "What does a dog know about mysteries?"

Then Billy yawned again and told us, "I'm not getting any sleep. Every night someone knocks on my door. When I ask who it is, no one answers. When I look outside, no one is there."

Billy's eyes began to close. My Dog poked him, and Billy told us more. "I hear those knocks a few times each night, but I never find anyone outside."

"Maybe it's a ghost," I said.

My Dog barked. I knew what she wanted.

"My Dog wants you to take us to your house. My Dog will solve your mystery."

As soon as Billy and I got up, My Dog picked up her toy bone. She began to play with it.

Billy laughed again. "Your dog is no detective. She poked me and barked because she wanted her bone."

"Come on," I called to My Dog. "This is no time to play. We have a mystery to solve."

My Dog dropped the bone and followed us to Billy's house.

Billy's house is small. I walked around it and looked for clues. While I was looking, My Dog sat under an apple tree. Some apples had fallen and My Dog was eating them.

"Come on," I called to My Dog. "This is no time to eat. We have a mystery to solve."

We walked around the house again and looked for clues. But there were none. The only footprints we found were ours.

"There are no clues out here," I told Billy. "We'll have to look inside."

I was about to go into the house when I noticed that My Dog wasn't with us. She was eating again.

"If you keep eating apples, you'll get sick," I told My Dog. "Now come and help me solve this mystery."

The rooms in Billy's house are all on the same level. I looked around. Everything was nice and neat. Just as we walked into Billy's room, we heard a knock.

"That's it!" Billy said.

We ran to the front door, but no one was there.

"That happens every night," Billy said. "I'm not getting any sleep."

"Well, it's not a ghost," I said. "Ghosts only knock at night."

I looked all around. I looked behind the bushes and trees. No one was hiding. I looked for fresh bicycle tracks, or car tracks. There were none.

"Why don't you ask your dog who is knocking on my door?" Billy said.

So I did. My Dog barked. She barked again.

"Your dog isn't smart," Billy said. "She's just noisy."

"Yes, she is smart," I said. "She wants me to ask you when you first heard a mystery knock."

"Oh, your dog doesn't want you to ask that," Billy said as he walked into his house. "All she wants to do is play and eat."

My Dog and I followed Billy inside. Just then, we heard another knock.

We ran outside and saw an apple roll off the roof and onto the ground. My Dog ran past us and bit into the apple.

"You'll get sick," I told My Dog. She looked at me and barked. Then she ate some more.

Just then I knew why My Dog was eating those apples. She was trying to tell me something. And I knew what it was.

"My Dog has done it again," I told Billy. "She's solved your mystery."

"All your dog has done," Billy said, "is eat my apples."

I walked over to the tree and shook it. Apples fell onto the roof.

I told Billy, "Your room is right under the tree. Every time an apple falls, you think someone is knocking. The only way to keep the apples from falling is to pick them all."

That's what we did. Billy and I picked every apple off the tree. And My Dog ate them.

I hope there are no mysteries to solve tomorrow. My Dog will be too sick to think!

Barry: The Dog Who Saved People

by Margaret Davidson
pictures by John Speirs

In this true dog story, a frightened girl is buried in the mountain snow. Only Barry, a brave rescue dog, can save her.

Today fine roads lead over the high mountains of Switzerland. Snowplows keep the roads open even in the worst weather. But it wasn't always this way.

Before the roads were built it was often very hard to cross over the mountains in winter. The only way was through some of the passes—pathways between the high peaks. One of these passes was called the Great St. Bernard Pass. At the highest point of the pass stood a big stone building. This was the monastery of Great St. Bernard. Monks had lived here for hundreds of years. They helped people travel safely in the mountains.

Sometimes the monks led travelers along the narrow path through the pass. And sometimes, when wild storms raged, they searched for those who might be lost.

This could be very dangerous work. But the monks had help. A group of big, shaggy dogs called St. Bernards also lived at the monastery. This is the story of one of those dogs. Barry was his name.

Barry was born in the spring of 1800. At first he romped and rolled with his brothers and sisters. He tagged after the bigger dogs. And he ate and slept whenever he felt like it.

But soon the short mountain summer was over. The first snow fell. It was time for Barry and the other young St. Bernards to go to school. They had some very important lessons to learn.

First Barry had to learn to obey. He learned to come when the monks called him, to sit and lie down when the monks told him to. He learned how to walk in the deep snow. He learned how to turn his big paws outward—and spread the pads of his paws to keep from sinking in the snow. At first he still sank in up to his belly. But after a while he could walk on the snowy crust without breaking through.

Now it was time for harder lessons. Barry learned to lead people through the pass even when the narrow path was buried under many feet of snow. And he learned one of the hardest lessons of all—to find people who might be lost in a storm.

If the person could walk, Barry led him back to the monastery. But sometimes a person would be hurt—or weakened by the cold. Then Barry raced back to the monastery to lead the monks back to the spot.

He learned to search for people who were lost under the snow. Sometimes an avalanche—a great slide of snow—would break free from one of the high peaks. It would come crashing down the mountain and bury anyone who was in its path.

The dogs were especially important at times like this. A dog could smell people even when they were buried under the snow. Then he would bark loudly, and the monks would come running.

All winter Barry and the other dogs learned their lessons. And before long the monks began to watch Barry very carefully. There was something special about the dog. He learned much faster than the others. But that was not enough. Would Barry also be brave? Could the monks trust him as a rescue dog?

At last the lessons were over, and Barry went to work. One afternoon he was trotting ahead of a long line of workmen, leading them through the pass. There was a loud booming noise. It was the beginning of an avalanche!

Barry had never heard this sound before. But somehow he knew that something terrible was about to happen. He raced ahead, barking. Then he circled back around the men. He was trying to get them to move faster. And the men tried. But the last three didn't make it. Moments later the avalanche rolled down over the trail—and the three men were buried under it.

They were probably still alive. It is possible to breathe under snow, but not for long.

Barry looked at the snowy spot for a moment. Then he bounded away. A few minutes later he dashed into the courtyard of the monastery. The monks came running when they heard his frantic barks. "It's trouble I can't handle alone!" those barks meant. "Follow me!" Then he started out into the snow again.

The monks followed Barry back to where the avalanche had slid across the path. And the men who had gotten through safely told them what had happened.

"Find them, Barry," a monk ordered. Barry began to sniff across the snow. Suddenly he barked. One of the monks ran over. Carefully he poked a long pole down into the snow. Nothing. He moved a few feet and poked again. Still nothing. So he tried a third time—and gave a shout. "Here!"

Other monks began to dig. A few minutes later the man was free. He was shivering and blue with cold, but he was alive! Soon the other two men were saved, too.

That night everyone—the monks and the rescued men—made a big fuss over Barry. They praised him. They petted him. They gave him a large bowl of juicy meat scraps. And the monks nodded to one another. They had been right. This was going to be a *very* special dog.

One day Barry was out on patrol. He saw a small mound of snow. Something was sticking out of that mound—something that looked like the end of a red scarf. Barry raced over. He saw now that the mound was a little girl! She lay curled up in the snow. Barry poked her. Was she still alive? She was. But the cold had made her very weak and sleepy.

Once more Barry seemed to know just what to do. He didn't run back to the monastery this time. He lay down beside the little girl instead. He half covered her with his warm, furry body. And he began to lick her face with his big, rough tongue.

At first the girl didn't move. But slowly as she grew warmer she began to stir. She snuggled under Barry's belly. And she opened her eyes.

She wasn't frightened. She knew right away the big dog was a friend. She continued to snuggle close to his side—and slowly his warmth woke her up. But she was still too weak to stand.

Barry looked around. It was very cold now. But when the sun went down it would be much, much colder.

Barry tugged at the girl's coat. He stood up. He lay down beside her again. It was as if he were telling her something. And maybe he was. Because now the little girl threw one leg around Barry's body. She

wrapped her arms around his furry neck. And a few minutes later the St. Bernard padded slowly into the courtyard of the monastery with the little girl riding on his back.

Stories like these soon made Barry famous on both sides of the mountains. Barry just went on doing his job. He did it for more than twelve years. And during that time he helped save the lives of forty-two people.

But the work was hard and the weather was harsh. Soon after Barry's twelfth birthday the monks noticed that the dog was growing stiff and slow.

Most old dogs were sent to homes in the warmer valleys below. But the monks couldn't bear to part with Barry. So he stayed at the monastery for several more years.

Then winter came once more. One wild and stormy night Barry was sleeping by the fire. There was a lull in the storm. The monks heard nothing. But Barry's ears were still sharp. Suddenly he was wide awake. He moved to the door and began to whine.

The monks thought he wanted to go into the courtyard. But when they opened the door Barry dashed away into the night.

Not far away Barry found what he was looking for — a man lying face downward in the snow. The man must have shouted a few minutes before. But now he lay very still with his eyes closed.

Barry bent over him. The man rolled over. He half opened his eyes. And what he saw made him scream. A big, dim shape was looming over him! "It's a wolf!" the man thought. With the last of his strength he pulled out a knife — and stuck it deep into Barry's side. Then he fainted again.

The old dog was badly wounded. But he still had a job to do. Somehow Barry got back to the monastery. He sank to the ground.

And the monks, lanterns held high, followed his paw prints — and drops of blood — back to the man.

They were in time to save the man's life. But no one was happy at the monastery that night. The monks took turns looking after Barry. At first they thought he would surely die. But finally he grew a little stronger.

Barry grew stronger, but he was never really well again. And he died a few months later.

The monks and the big St. Bernards still live in the high mountains of Switzerland. But life at the monastery is very different now. Far below, a tunnel goes through the mountain. And a safe road has been built through the pass nearby.

So the dogs are no longer needed for rescue work. But Barry has not been forgotten. Every few years an especially lively and intelligent pup is born at the monastery. That pup is always named Barry.

TICK-TOCK-WOOF!

Jokes and Riddles

TICK-TOCK-WOOF!

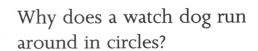

What animal goes
tick-tock-woof?

A watch dog.

Why does a watch dog run
around in circles?

To wind himself up.

What time is it when ten German
shepherds are running after two poodles?

Ten after two.

DOGTOR, DOGTOR!

Where do you take a sick dog?

To the dogtor.

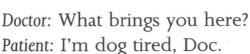

Doctor: What brings you here?
Patient: I'm dog tired, Doc.
Doctor: I think you should see a veterinarian.

Psychiatrist: What's on
    your mind?
Patient: I think I'm a dog.
Psychiatrist: How long has
    this been going on?
Patient: Ever since I was a puppy.

Patient: I was bitten on the leg by a dog.
Doctor: Did you put anything on it?
Patient: No. He liked it just the way it was.

CALLING ALL DOGS!

What do you call a dog
with the flu?

A germy shepherd.

What do you call a dog who
likes to fight?

A boxer.

What do you call a dog who just
arrived in the Big Apple?

A New Yorkie.

What do you call a hungry dog?

A chow hound.

What do you call Dracula's dog?

A bloodhound.

What do you call a dog that weighs 600 pounds,
with razor-sharp teeth and an attitude problem?

Don't call him anything—run!

WHY, DOG?

Why did the dog go to the beach?

He wanted to be a hot dog!

Why is a dog so hot in the summer?

Because he wears a fur coat and pants.

Why does a dog wear a fur coat?

If he didn't he'd be a little bear.

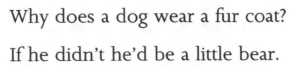

WHAT, DOG?

What's white, with black and red spots?

A Dalmatian with the measles.

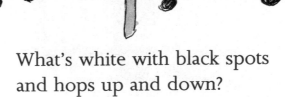

What's white with black spots
and hops up and down?

A Dalmatian with the hiccups.

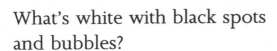

What's white with black spots
and bubbles?

A Dalmatian taking a bubble bath.

KNOCK-KNOCK . . .

Knock-knock.
Who's there?
Pecan.
Pecan who?
Pecan a dog
your own size.

Knock-knock.
Who's there?
Mandy.
Mandy who?
Man, dese fleas are itching me!

Knock-knock.
Who's there?
Sherwood.
Sherwood who?
Sherwood like a nice bone to chew.

Knock-knock.
Who's there?
Anybody.
Anybody who?
Anybody going to walk the dog?

PUPPIES!

What do dogs have
that no other animals have?

Puppies!

Which dogs are the quietest?

Hush puppies.

What is a puppy after
she's five months old?

Six months old.

GIVE A DOG
A BONE

Tail Ends

THE BOW-WOW
BOOKSHOP

Best-sellers for Dogs

102 Dalmatians
by Seymour Spotz

Lassie, Stay Hom
by Tyer Upp

Home Alone
by Chew N. D'Chaire

How to Raise Dachshunds
by Frank Furter

Canine Cookbook
by O. Penn Accan

Puddles on the Floor
by Ima Puppy

Best Bones for Dogs
by A. Skeleton

HOT DOGS
FOR SALE
A Rebus Story

One ☀️ 🦵 day a 👧 was walking her 🐕 on a 🦮 . The 🐕 pulled. The 🦮 broke. The 🐕 ran away. Sniff! Sniff! The 🐕 wiggled his 👃 . He smelled 🌭-s. The 🌭-s were in a 🚐 . The 🐕 jumped into the 🚐 . The 🚐 began to go. "Woof! Woof!" said the 🐕

The [car] stopped at a [traffic light].

The [dog] could hear his [girl]. She

said, "May [eye] have a [hot dog], please?"

She gave [dollar] [2] the [man].

The [man] gave her a [hot dog].

Just then the [dog] jumped out of the

[car].

"How about that?" said the [girl]. "[eye]

got [2] dogs for the price of [1]!"

SHOULD YOU REALLY GIVE A DOG A BONE?

Facts About Dogs

Should You Really Give a Dog a Bone?
It depends on the kind of bone.
Many bones can splinter and hurt your
dog. Better check with your vet first.

How Well Can Dogs Smell?
Very, very well. Some dogs can
detect the scent of a person's
fingerprint six weeks after it was made!

Does Your Dog Have Good Eyes?
Not really. Dogs are color-blind. They
see the world in shades of gray. And
things don't look sharp and clear to
a dog. If your dog were a person, he
would probably be wearing glasses!

Does a Wagging Tail Mean a Dog Is Friendly?
Not always. Depending on the
position and the way it is moving, a
wagging tail may mean different
things. The dog could be friendly,
frightened, or even ready to fight.

Why Do Dogs Bark "at Nothing"?

They don't! Dogs have such good ears that they can hear sounds that are four times farther away than those a person can hear. When your dog barks "at nothing," she probably hears something you don't.

Does Your Dog Have More Than One Fur Coat?

Yes! Most dogs have *two* coats! The outer coat is made of long hairs. The undercoat is made of short, fluffy hairs. The undercoat is like long underwear and keeps the dog warm in the winter. When the weather warms up, the undercoat falls out.

Can Dogs Stand on Their Toes?

Yes. As a matter of fact, dogs are always standing on their toes—unless they are lying down. A dog's foot is built so the heel is high up and the toes are on the ground. This helps the dog run faster.

TITLE INDEX

AUTHOR AND ARTIST INDEX